E   R326639
Iwa   8.95
Iwamura
Ton and Pon: two good friends

DATE DUE			
MR 27 '85	FE 20 '86	JY 29 '88	
AP 18 '85	MR 28 '86	AG 18 '88	
MY 21 '85	AP 11 '86	FE 16 '89	
JY 6 '85	AP 15 '86	JY 29 '90	
	AP 29 '86	AG 30 '90	
AG 1 '85	JE 27 '86		
AG 3 '85	OC 1 '87		
	DE 28 '87		
AG 27 '85			
SE 19 '85	FE 1 '88		
JA 6 '85	MR 21 '88		
JA 28 '86	JY 15 '88		

EB

TON and PON

and

Two Good Friends

By Kazuo Iwamura

Bradbury Press   Scarsdale, N.Y.

Today is Mickie's birthday.
"Why don't you two take her
these nice red apples," said Big Ton's mother.
"And don't fight along the way," said Little Pon's mother.

"Let's play rocks, scissors, paper.
The loser has to carry the basket."

"Okay."

"One, two, three.
Paper covers stone. I win!"

"These apples are too heavy."

"What a fine day for a walk."

"I've had my turn long enough.
Let's play rock, scissors, paper again.
Look. Scissors cuts paper. I win."

"Too heavy for you, Pon?"

"Working together is easier, isn't it, Ton?

"Yes, much easier."

"I have a plan."

"Isn't this better?"

"Much better."

"Isn't this a good idea?"

"A really good idea."

"Well, now this really is a good idea."

"A very good idea."

"Now here's an idea that works."

"Yes, it does, doesn't it?"

"I can't go another step."

"Me either."

"Here's the best idea of the day."

"Excellent."

"No more heavy apples."

"But what will we give to Mickie?"
"Well . . ."

"Absolutely the top idea of all."

"Yes, isn't it."

"So easy to carry."

"Beautiful flowers for Mickie."

"Happy Birthday, Mickie."

What pretty flowers."
Thank you, Big Ton and Little Pon."

"We're so glad you came.
Here are some lovely apples
to take home to your mothers."

Bradbury Press, Inc.
2 Overhill Road, Scarsdale, N.Y. 10583
An affiliate of Macmillan, Inc.
Collier Macmillan Canada, Inc.
Manufactured in the United States of America. First American edition published by Bradbury Press, Inc., 1984.
10 9 8 7 6 5 4 3 2 1
The text of this book is set in 18 pt. Aster.
Library of Congress Cataloging in Publication Data
Iwamura, Kazuo, 1939–
    Ton and Pon: two good friends.
    Translation of: Ton to Pon: ii kangae desho.
    Summary: Sharing the carrying of a heavy basket to a friend inspires Ton and Pon, two young dogs, to find a way to lighten it.
    [1. Dogs—Fiction.   2. Stories without words]   I. Title.
PZ7.I954Tq   1984   [E]   83-22345   ISBN 0-02-747510-7